ᴛhe
ᴍᴀᴦɪc
ᴦʀoᴠe

A Persian Folktale
Retold by Libuše Paleček
Illustrated by Josef Paleček

PICTURE BOOK STUDIO USA

Copyright © 1985, Verlag Neugebauer Press, Salzburg.
Original title: DER ZAUBERHAIN
Copyright © 1985, English text, Neugebauer Press USA, Inc.
Published in USA by Picture Book Studio USA,
an imprint of Neugebauer Press USA, Inc.
Distributed by Alphabet Press, Natick, MA.
Distributed in Canada by Vanwell Publishing, St. Catharines, Ont.
Published in U.K. by Neugebauer Press Publishing Ltd., London.
Distributed by A & C Black PLC., London.
Distributed in Australia by Hutchinson Group Australia Pty. Ltd.
Printed in Austria.

LIBRARY OF CONGRESS CATALOGING IN PUBLICATION DATA

Paleček, Libuše.
The magic grove.

Translation of: Der Zauberhain.
Summary: A retelling of a traditional Persian tale in
which a kind act is rewarded in a very special way.
[1. Folklore — Iran] I. Paleček, Josef, ill. II. Title.
PZ8.1.P18Mag   1984   398.2'42'0955   84-26533
ISBN 0-907234-72-0

Once there lived two true friends, somewhere on the wide rolling savannah of a faraway country.

One of them farmed a little field and was all alone except for his daughter Ubiana. They worked from dawn to sunset every day, plowing and planting and watering their crops.

The other, also a widower, lived nearby and grazed a small herd of sheep with his son Asan. They tended their flock carefully, and once each year they sheared off the wool and sold it. The rest of the time they made cheese from the milk, and occasionally they would have a fine sheepskin to sell in the marketplace in the distant city of the great Khan.

The farmer and the shepherd were not rich, but there was always enough, and when good friends share what little they have, it seems like a lot.

Their children had played together since childhood, and both fathers were happy to see that as Asan and Ubiana grew up, their childish fondness for one another turned into a new, shy feeling, full of timid and gentle courtesies.

So all four of them lived in love and friendship, quietly, simply, and contentedly.

But then came the summer of the great drought.
Every day a burning fireball rolled across the sky, and the earth
cracked beneath its merciless glow.

The sun burned up the farmer's crops, and even the hardiest grasses
of the savannah withered away to nothing. The water in the well sank
low and there was no rain, not even a cloud.

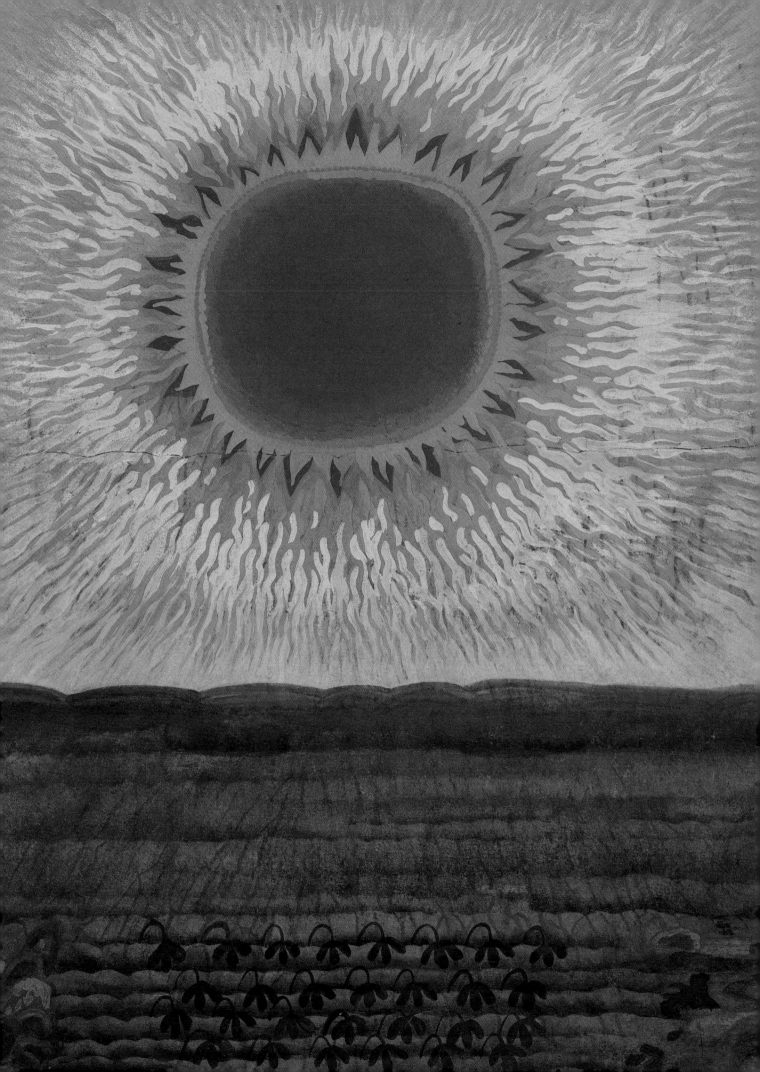

The shepherd's flock was left without any food, and every last one of his sheep died of hunger and thirst.

One noon, when the only sound in the deathly stillness was the crackle of the fire as it burned the sheep carcasses, they all stiffened in fright. As if matters were not bad enough already, an even greater danger was sweeping across the savannah.

They charged like a whirlwind!

Without even dismounting, the Khan's horsemen trampled the fields, shattered the shepherd's yurta, and seized everything they could lay hands on. Just as suddenly, they wheeled their horses about and thundered away, leaving behind only destruction, confusion, and the fear that they might return.

The shepherd and Asan lost everything. They had nothing left to eat, and no money to buy more sheep.

But then the farmer, who was a little better off, said to his friend: "For many years I have shared my heart with you. Now I shall also share my bread with you. You cannot refuse this."

That same day they brought the remains of the shepherd's yurta to the farmer's land and decided that they would all farm together.

When they had mended the shepherd's home and set it up near the farmhouse, the farmer gave tools to each of them and they started to prepare the soil for the new sowing. Since there were four of them working together now, they were able to enlarge the little field and make it as big as it was when Ubiana's great grandfather had farmed the land.

One day, when Asan's father was clearing a new bit of field, he dug up a pot full of golden coins. He realized at once that he had found the family treasure, buried here long ago. Delighted, he ran to give it to his friend. But the farmer would not accept the treasure.
"The gifts of the earth belong to him who waters it with his sweat. You did the work, the earth rewarded you. The treasure is yours!"
"This bit of ground has always been cultivated by your ancestors. It is your land and your treasure." said the shepherd, pressing the gold on his friend. But the farmer did not agree.

The two men argued on and on about what should belong to whom, and they passed the heavy pot of money back and forth again and again. Finally the shepherd, whose arms were getting tired, put an end to the discussion: he made a gift of the treasure to Ubiana.

The farmer knew instantly what to do. He took his dear daughter and, together with the pot of gold, he gently pushed her into the arms of Asan.

And that was that! What joy there was! What kisses and hugs!

Pr

FICTION MICHENER
    Personal Author:
    Title: Recession
   copy:1
library:WEST_E
location:ADULT

FICTION MILLER
    Personal Author:
    Title: The killer

   copy:1
library:WEST_E
location:ADULT

FICTION MINER
    Personal Author:
    Title: Range of l
   copy:1
library:WEST_E
location:ADULT

Produ

FICTION MITCHARD
    Personal Author: Mi
    Title: The deep end
   copy:1

PCH

The secret wish that Asan and Ubiana had shared for so long came true. They received their fathers' blessing and were married that very day. The two fathers set up house together in the shepherd's yurta, so that the young couple could have the farmhouse to themselves.

Amid all the excitement and happiness of the day, the treasure was forgotten. Shortly after dark the shepherd remembered, and brought the pot of gold into the yurta.

Early next morning the old men hurried into the house to give the treasure to their children. But to their surprise, Asan and Ubiana refused it too. They had their love and wished for nothing more.

So what was to be done with the gold?

They could buy a flock of sheep in the market...
But if the drought returned the sheep would only suffer and die.

Or they could buy many rare and precious objects...
But what's the use of such things here?

What about buying a stone house in the city...
But who would give up the freedom of the wide savannah for the town with the Khan and his cruelty? What did they lack that they did not have right here?

If only the drought were not so fierce! But you cannot screen off the sun with gold, and rain cannot be summoned with money.

As they all sat thinking silently, Ubiana's eyes came to rest upon the old carpet hanging behind them with its picture of a beautiful shady grove. "That is how we can use the gold!" she said gaily.
When the others saw where she was pointing, they understood immediately. Of course! Give the treasure back to the land. They would buy the most precious young seedlings and plant a grove of deep-rooted trees. And when the trees grew, they would protect the people and the land from the sun.

And so Asan set out for the Khan's city with the treasure. He knew the way well. Many times he had made this journey with his father to sell cheese and wool and skins in the market. But now he went alone.

On and on he traveled.
First through the steppe, then through drier land where the tufts of
hard, spiky grass grew ever thinner and more dwarfed, and then
through brushlands bitter with the scent of wormwood.

By night, Asan slept wherever he could find a little shelter.
Only the moon kept him company...
and the stars,
and the silence,
and his own fear.

At last he reached his goal.

At the wall of the town he found a little stall. There, in soft baskets and round precious seeds their shady grove was waiting.

He had picked out the finest plants and seeds with his eyes, and he was ready to buy, when a strange and plaintive song fell on his ears. A long caravan approached from the desert, and every camel carried several cages filled with exotic birds.

Asan hurried toward them and then stood and stared, enchanted by their beauty. Where might birds like this live? Where were they being taken? And why did their little throats give forth such touching tones, like helpless weeping? To his horror he learned that they were on their way to be killed for the Khan's banquet table.

Asan could not believe his ears — were these splendid birds never again to fly free? He ran ahead of the caravan, trying to stop it, but the camel-driver ignored him. The caravan plodded on.

Again Asan ran ahead, stopped, hesitated, and then decided.
When the scorching sun reflected the glitter of gold, the caravan
stopped. Asan offered his treasure in exchange for the birds' freedom.

In just a moment, the desert was covered with cages, each one filled with birds who chirped impatiently for their freedom. Excitedly he opened their little prisons and they eagerly took to the air.

The sky was bright, filled with color and birdsongs. The birds circled happily over Asan a few times and then flew off into the distance. Long after they had disappeared from sight, their beautiful songs floated back to him through the clear desert air.

Asan set out on his homeward journey with a light heart. But as he walked and walked, his enchantment began to seep away. His feet grew heavy and he became gloomy. Should he return at all? How could he come home empty-handed, with no precious seeds and no treasure?

Could he face them after they had sweated under the burning sun to prepare the field for their new shady grove? When they ran out to meet him, Asan told them everything — all about the caged birds on their way to certain death at the Khan's court, and their return to life. He confessed the price he had paid for their freedom. Face to face with the two old men and his beloved Ubiana, he felt very guilty.

But there was not a word of reproach. They were not angry with Asan, for they knew that they would have done the same. They were free people of the savannah. That evening they spoke at length of Asan's journey, of the wonderful exotic birds, and of the strange, distant world where some people make a living by taking from others.

At dusk they all went home except the farmer, who paused to think, staring at the place where the grove would have been. Picking up a shovel, he slowly filled in one of the holes and then went into the yurta.

The shepherd wasn't asleep either. He was thinking of his son and the wonderful trees they would have planted the next day. The old men lay down without a word. They had often talked together and shared their hopes for a cool and shady grove on the wide savannah, but now each had to bury his own dreams alone. It was a long time before sleep came to give them a rest from all their unhappy thoughts.

Ubiana also sat up late into the night, looking at delicate bird feathers, a gift from Asan. In her mind's eye she saw the sad and beautiful pictures he had described for them.

Only Asan slept calmly and contentedly.

In the middle of the night there came a sound like the wind. The air was filled with the rustling wings of birds, and each one carried a little sprig in its beak. As the birds planted the leafy twigs, the small branches stretched up, growing and pushing out more and more leaves. The fluttering of wings and the growing of the young trees filled the night air with busy whispers. Finished with their work, the birds settled down to rest and sang their most cheerful songs while they waited for the dawn.

Asan sat straight up in bed and listened. Jumping up, he rushed outside into the morning light. He could not believe his eyes! Was it real, or was it a dream, or a miracle? Suddenly his eyes were full of tears. He realized it was a gift — a great, unexpected, beautiful gift.

In all his life on the savannah, he had never seen so many trees! Last night there was just a field covered with holes, and now a grove of beautiful trees spread their roots deep into the earth and reached strong branches into the sky. And in every tree sat singing birds — the very ones Asan had rescued! Seeing him, the birds sang even louder.

Ubiana and the two fathers came running out into the grove to feast their eyes on the incredible beauty. Above them the birds circled happily, greeted them, and then settled in silence onto the trees. Into the silence came the gurgle of water. On the spot where the shepherd had found the treasure, a spring of clear, cold water burbled up from underground. The birds drank from it thirstily, and the people drank too. Ubiana bent down and put her hands into the cool water, and then splashed it about happily. Wherever the drops fell onto the trees, they burst into flower. One after another the trees lit up with glowing blossoms, and the grove rang with laughter and birdsongs.

But suddenly the birdsongs stopped.

The Khan's raiders galloped across the savannah, and pulled up
sharply in front of the grove. The soldiers aimed their arrows and
tried to shoot, but the terrible shrieking of the birds frightened the
horses, and they reared up and danced nervously on their back legs.
Whipping their horses and shouting curses, the horsemen drew their
swords and rushed toward the grove.

Suddenly, the low bushes and thorny vines seemed to jump towards the legs of the horses, grabbing and tearing at them. The horsemen screamed with fear and retreated in a cloud of dust.

As the hoofbeats faded in the distance, there was a moment of deep silence, this time full of relief. Then the birds and the people burst out into happy cheers — glad, and grateful, and safe at last.

They say it was the wind who spread the news of a magic grove, hidden somewhere deep in the savannah, a place with green grasses and plenty of water — a place where the Khan's hordes were frightened to go. People started to pour in from far and near, but not all of them were welcomed. Only those with good intentions were invited to live and work in this wonderful place.

It is said that even to this day their children and grandchildren and great-grandchildren are still there. Their lives are like a true fairy tale, for nothing holds back their happiness, and they have nothing to fear.